Jackie Lewis was born in Preston in 1959. After spending many years travelling around the south of England, as well as a short stint in Ireland and the South of France, in 1993 she returned up north to Manchester with her daughter.

She studied English Literature at City College in Manchester and has, through her wealth of experience in a variety of different jobs from barmaid to carer to medical secretary, always fed her writing with the complex psychology of a multitude of characters.

After more than twenty years of writing in stolen hours, this is her first collection of short stories.

The Dropped Baby
and other curious tales

JACKIE LEWIS

The Dropped Baby
and other curious tales

Vanguard Press

VANGUARD PAPERBACK

© Copyright 2015
Jackie Lewis

A CIP catalogue record for this title is
available from the British Library.

ISBN 978 178465 034 6

Vanguard Press is an imprint of
Pegasus Elliot Mackenzie Publishers Ltd.
www.pegasuspublishers.com

First Published in 2015

Vanguard Press
Sheraton House Castle Park
Cambridge England

Printed & Bound in Great Britain

To Margot, Briony and David
With all my love.

Acknowledgements

I want to thank my daughter, Briony, for her patience and for always believing in me. Thank you to Tina, for constant support, friendship and fun. David, your encouragement and support has been instrumental in getting me to this point. Thank you all!

With grateful thanks also to Michael Atkins for providing the original artwork.

Contents

Read to capture the mind; write to free the spirit

—Daveedo, 25 January 2015

Dolls' House

'No one has seen him for over a week now,' Susie's gossipy voice continued down the phone line, beginning to irritate Lindsay slightly. Much as she loved her friend, she really could talk the hind leg off a donkey!

Susie was talking about old Mr Jones from further down the same street, who lived at No 60 and who had, according to her, apparently 'just disappeared' sometime over the last week. Lindsay, keeping one eye on her daughter Samantha, who sat on the floor – her doll's house open before her, half its contents spread out around her – patiently let her friend rattle on a bit longer before finishing the call with a promise of coffee later in the week. She had so much to do and Tim would be home soon! She hadn't even started to think about what to have for tea.

Later that evening, sitting on the floor, Samantha on her knee, Lindsay had a few quiet moments to consider what really might have happened to Mr Jones, poor old chap. She did hope he was all right; she had quite liked him on the rare occasions she had passed by his little front garden and stopped for a chat. He was a really old fashioned little man, with round, polished reading glasses perched on the end of his nose, and he always clutched a wooden pipe in one hand.

In fact, it was thanks to him Samantha had the doll's house she so loved playing with, as it was old Mr Jones that had put them in touch with a relative selling one. Perhaps he would just turn up again; perhaps he had been to visit a relative somewhere out of the town and just not bothered to tell the neighbours? That was the thing about having a neighbour like Susie – not much got past her! Lindsay felt confident she would no doubt be getting a further 'bulletin' on the situation before too long.

The dolls' house had just about everything now: every room filled with tiny chairs and tables, lamps and stripy carpets, even miniature portraits hanging on the walls. Everything except people. Lindsay thought that perhaps Susie would know where she could buy some. It was Sam's fifth birthday next month and she knew her daughter would love to have some little people to 'play house' with.

Coffee and conversation in full flow, Lindsay remembered to ask her friend where she could buy some figures for the doll's house and, of course, Susie knew.

Sarah Winter was the best bet as she had a market stall in the town every Saturday and apparently stocked all sorts of things, including dolls' house items and sometimes miniature figures too. Susie took full advantage of this by informing Lindsay that she also happened to know that Sarah was what was known as a modern day witch… in that she dabbled in herbalism. According to her gossipy friend, Sarah Winter came from a long line of herbalists and had always had that strange look about her. 'In fact', she went on, Sarah and old Mr Jones were neighbours not that long ago and they fell out big style. 'Perhaps', Susie rattled on, Sarah had magicked old Jones away somehow! Lindsay suppressed a laugh at the thought of this woman, Sarah Winter, waving her arms manically about her head and turning old Mr Jones into a can of baked beans

Saturday morning found Lindsay wandering amongst the many colourful stalls in the market place: fruit and vegetables, second hand books, cake stands, sewing materials and there tucked into a far corner was Sarah Winter's stall. She knew it must have been the right one because the table top was literally covered in dolls' furniture and stacks and stacks of little white boxes.

Lindsay approached the stall and smiled at the soft leathery face that greeted her from under a woollen cap. She did look a bit eccentric, but a witch? After a few pleasantries, Lindsay explained what she was looking for and Sarah happily got box after box out for her to look at and inspect, explaining how she herself had made all the intricate dresses and shirts for the miniature dolls house people. They really were marvellous thought Lindsay as she touched the tiny lace cuffs of the mother figure and the crisp linen of the father's jacket.

She decided on a mother, a father and two children figures. She also asked Sarah if she could possibly find a butler figure and perhaps a gardener too, as the dolls' house had a patch of green attached to it at the back which was presumably meant to be a garden. To her delight Sarah said she could supply both. So without opening these last two purchases – as they were bound to be just as professional as the others – Lindsay added these to her other items for Sarah to gift wrap. This she happily did, complete with a large silver box and blue ribbon thrown in free.

As soon as she got home Lindsay undid the packages to take another look before wrapping them up again, using the special birthday paper ready for Sam's big day. She studied the minute detail of the clothes and marvelled again at the intricate work that must have gone into them; they really did almost look real.

She heard the familiar plop of the local newspaper hit the hall mat and went through to retrieve it before the dog did. Glancing at the front page she saw a black and white photograph of old Mr Jones' face with a large caption underneath it which read "Have you seen this man?" So it was true, he really was missing then, she thought sadly.

Turning her attention back to the last two unopened boxes she held out the 'butler'. Complete with smart pinstriped suit and white tie, there was even a tiny silver tray in one hand. Then the very last figure – the gardener. To her delight he even had a tiny pair of round glasses and a tiny wooden pipe clutched in one hand, perfect. She wrapped them all up again and went into the kitchen to start the evening meal.

Too Much To Bear

The rows and rows of tiny eyes all seemed to be watching him as Maurice slowly took another sip of his claret, settled deep back into his chair and stared back at them from his own small 'black as coal' eyes. With a sudden shiver he stood up and strode across the now darkening room to slam shut the sash cord window that was letting in the chill of the early evening. His long legs aching with sitting in one position for too long, Maurice raised his slender arms and stretched long fingers above his white feathery head in an indulgent stretch to bring the blood flowing back.

The room stood quietly, glinting glass display cabinets and highly polished wood lining two walls of the small room, and each of these in turn sat stuffed to overflowing with miniature porcelain animals. Most were bears of some kind, perfectly formed in minute detail, the more dominant polar bears with glistening coats, their yellow teeth set in wildly open mouths that had never breathed in life. Some stood up on hind legs, raised paws swiping at invisible fish, caught forever in the moment; others sat up, slept or appeared to be running. All now sat under a gathering layer of dust. Tut tut thought Maurice, what would Kathleen have said?

Grotesque, thought Maurice, simply grotesque, each and every one of them. What on earth could she possibly have got from them, he mused, stroking his beard and shaking his head. It truly was beyond him. They somehow reminded him of the huge guard dogs his father had kept in the back yard, with their bared yellow teeth and that unapproachable look in their eye, and it made him shiver with the memory.

He settled back down in his chair, resting long slender hands on its worn leather arms and stretched his legs out carefully in front of him. His top lip curled in quiet contentment, one of his rarer moments, as he liked to think of them. Moments when he felt he was in control. He began to slowly scan the porcelain figures once again, trying to decide which one he would destroy next.

When he had met Kathleen some eight years before, he had been fast approaching his fiftieth birthday and had concluded that a wife was perhaps something he would have to do without. Maurice had always thought of women as 'rather difficult' and had not enjoyed much success with the opposite sex over the years, so when Kathleen appeared in his life it had come as rather a surprise. Not only was she reasonably intelligent, she was also quite timid, dressed 'sensibly', was capable of putting a decent meal together and also quite easy on the eye. She was very short with mousy brown hair and had small neat features set in a thin pale face. An only child, she had moved into the area a year ago – had never married.

Maurice decided that as she would not disrupt his world too much he would marry her. It did not occur to him that she could possibly say no when he proposed within two months of meeting her. As predicted, she accepted and Kathleen moved quietly into his large flat with just a few boxes of possessions, mostly her collection of porcelain bears.

At first it hadn't been a problem. Maurice dismissed her slightly puzzling hobby as 'something that women did' – have hobbies, make things, collect things, and so on. What mattered now was that he had a wife in place to help stabilise his life. There would be a hot meal on the table at the end of his long day in the bank and the flat would be cleaned regularly. She was almost without character and would be easy to manipulate – most agreeable.

As time passed however, Maurice came to realise just how much of an obsession Kathleen's 'little hobby' was turning out to be. Where once there would have been a hot meal almost ready, or even actually on the table as he walked through the door from a long day's work, he more and more often came back to nothing, except finding his wife down on her hands and knees; yet again, in front of the damn cabinets polishing and dusting her precious ever-growing collection of ornaments. Worse still she was usually completely oblivious to him!

Maurice knew his wife now spent time – a lot of her free time – with one of the neighbours, a small wittery looking blonde woman who lived alone in the basement flat and he rather resented that too. She was his wife damn it and she was beginning to neglect him. She was obviously spending the house keeping money he gave her on more and more ornaments whilst the dishes lay untouched, piled up in the kitchen sink. Maurice felt more and more irritated, more and more cheated from what he saw as 'his side of the deal'. It wasn't acceptable.

Kathleen always obeyed her husband quickly, getting up from her crouched position on the floor, head bowed, covering her ears from her husband's angry raised voice, as she hurried into the kitchen to start the dinner under the silent spiteful burn of her husband's eyes.

It had been a particularly long and trying day at work, Maurice had entered the small front room wearily – difficult meetings with the executors, even talk of possible redundancies. He felt utterly exhausted, irritated and most of all ravenously hungry. So, the sight of his wife, yet again sitting on her heels, hair scraped back into a tight bun, elbows moving frantically in and out as she polished away as if in some silent and very private world of her own, was just too much to bear.

Shaking with rage, Maurice lunged at the open cabinet, exacting a terrified howl from the kneeling figure of his wife as she frantically rolled out of the way of his long bony hands. Grabbing indiscriminately at the hateful objects, he flung the bears all over the floor and with a rising outrage, blowing shades of purple into his pale face, he raised his foot high and slammed it down as hard as he could, sending fine shards of polished china in every direction. Kathleen sat horrified on the floor, tears rolling freely down her thin crumpled face, small fists clenched tightly into each other in disbelief. She wanted to kill him in that moment but was so afraid of him that she dared not even meet his gaze, gasping in horror as Maurice took another handful of ornaments out of the cabinet. She watched him hurl them against the wall just behind her head and she began to cower. The ghastly cracking metallic sound of splintering china drove home the absolute fury Kathleen now felt. But she had closed her eyes, given up, too afraid to even move now, in case he decided to hurl her against the wall too and perhaps shatter her very bones into splinters.

She waited for the sounds in the room to return to normal, eyes still tight shut, trying to stabilise her breathing; but all she could hear was her husband's deep indignant breaths as he paced the room, the oh so familiar rattle from his constricted throat that he made when his temper got the better of him.

That night she cried herself to sleep whilst a cold and completely indifferent Maurice lay with his back to her. He had told her, before putting the lamp out and in no uncertain tones that she had to choose, him or the bears. He told her that he would not tolerate this 'nonsense' of hers any longer; he needed a wife that would look after *his* needs.

Strange now, thought Maurice, here he was all alone with the very cause of his grief, the roots of his anger, and yet he felt in no hurry to destroy them. Perhaps he mused, two long fingers gently stroking his beard, it would be much more pleasurable to take his time. What was that saying, about revenge being a dish best served cold? He chuckled softly to himself and adjusted his chair, slowly folding one long leg out over the other, careful not to cause a crease in his expensive linen trousers.

Now then, which one would be next? Yes, scratching their surfaces with the very tip of his penknife was in fact particularly satisfying. Pouring himself another large claret he glanced towards the bathroom door. He had made quite a good job of it, all in all, he thought to himself, flashes of colour and screaming passing briefly across his conscience. Just a new carpet in there and that would be that. He made a mental note to destroy one of the larger bears next that sat dominating the upper shelf of the nearest cabinet – perhaps he would drop it out of the bathroom window?

The next evening, just as Maurice had the ornament condemned the night before, halfway out of the bathroom window still dangling from his bony fingertips, his doorbell rang. Biting his lip in irritation he put the bear down inside the bath and controlling his annoyance made his way to the front door. He didn't have many visitors as a rule, so opening his door slowly found himself staring down into the timid face of the wittery blonde from the basement, Kathleen's 'friend', Alice.

Ah, thought Maurice, small expressionless eyes staring down at her, Kathleen's confidante, come to find out what's what no doubt. If she hadn't spent so much time with her, enjoying their daily character assassination of him, then perhaps his wife would have put more thought into seeing to his needs.

He forced a "yes?" out, to which the nervous little woman asked if it was a bad time, and that she could come back but she wanted a quick word with Kathleen, please, if that was all right. She smelled strongly of perfume and wore a smartly tailored skirt suit. Independent type, Maurice judged, probably single, more trouble than they are worth.

Suddenly tired of what he saw now as a silly game he practically barked at her, "Kathleen and I have parted company; you may as well know now – that she no longer lives at this address."

Before Alice could take in this information the door had been slammed in her perplexed face. Shocked at his sudden and totally unprovoked violent outburst, she stood still for several seconds before turning suddenly on her heel and heading back downstairs to her flat.

Oh, she had known about Maurice all right. The man was by all accounts a pig who always got his own way by bullying and manipulating poor Kathleen. She had seen for herself now why the poor love was always such a mess. She had seen her crying over copious cups of tea in her basement because of his outbursts of temper – but split up? Left him? This wasn't right. Kathleen would never have found the courage to leave him and would have told her first for sure. No, this wasn't right.

When she got up the next day Alice thought long and hard about Kathleen's 'disappearance' because this in effect was what it amounted to. She also felt a growing sense of unease about the whole situation; Maurice's outburst had been completely unreasonable, possibly even defenceless? She would have to try and find out some answers, she knew, as she stood at her kitchen sink, peering through the small window which was just above the ground level.

As she stood there she suddenly saw Maurice cross the road in front of the flats and stand by the bus stop on the other side of the road.

That's odd, she thought. What was he doing catching a bus when he had a car and why wasn't the control freak in work anyway at ten o'clock in the morning? Kathleen had told her enough times about him being a stickler for routine; he left for work at exactly eight forty-five a.m. and arrived at nine thirty a.m., precisely. This was certainly out of character.

Later in the day she saw him again, returning, leaving the bus and quickly crossing the road back to the flats, hat and coat on one arm a small hold all in the other.

The next day she rang in sick at the Library, fabricating food poisoning and decided this was her chance to do something. She was ready for him this time, though she found herself pacing anxiously up and down the small kitchen, willing him to appear. He finally came out just before ten and strolled across the road to the bus stop again, just as he had done the day before. She decided she would follow him. She ran for the stairs and up out across the lawns and the road to the bus stop, just as the bus pulled out. Damn it, she hissed under her breath. Now she would have to wait for the next one or try again tomorrow.

Realising how futile getting the next No 47 bus would have been – to where for God's sake? She decided to try again the next day. She would have to be sick another day.

This time she had a heavy woollen scarf round her face and held well back in the bus queue – luckily three others had also been waiting this time and Maurice was standing at the other end of the line and had not noticed her.

They boarded the bus and she got just close enough to hear him ask for the zoo as his destination – the bloody zoo? What was that all about? she thought. A grown man, going to the zoo on his own? She practically whispered to the driver when it came to her turn to pay her fare and quickly took a seat on the lower deck of the bus, having seen Maurice take the stairs to the upper deck. She sat miserably on the plastic covered seat, feeling the heat build up behind her knees, eyes pinned on the stairwell. The bus heaved itself on and on bumping over uneven patches of road skirting the town centre, engine complaining loudly under the strain.

He suddenly emerged from the stairwell, long legs appearing before the rest of him, followed by a swirling overcoat and his holdall under one arm. She averted her face, pretending to stare out of the window until she could wait no longer and once again ran for the doors, collecting an angry glance from the driver for jumping off at the last minute. It took her a few minutes to realise where she was but sure enough peering ahead of her she could just make out the sign that said City Zoo – it *was* the zoo.

She watched him approach the entrance and pay his way in before allowing the sinking feeling inside her well up to form large frustrated tears that wet her face, as she turned away and back towards the buses. What a fool, she thought, to think this would lead me to Kathleen. The man must be completely without conscience, his marriage has broken down and here he was appearing like someone enjoying a nice day out to the zoo with his lunch in a holdall no doubt. He just didn't care, that much was now obvious; the man really was a monster. Her only saving grace was that he had not seen her and with this small gratitude in her mind she started for home.

Maurice walked through the compounds of the large noisy zoo, past the brightly coloured birds, the tropical fish in the aquariums, the ring tailed monkeys. He didn't stop to look at anything, he was far too preoccupied with his innermost thoughts. He continued to walk onwards until at last he saw the beginnings of the high black railings. With a growing sense of excitement, lifting his heart in mood, he moved closer to the railings until he stood with one hand on a high black rail and the other clutching his holdall.

Leaning closer he stared down into the murky grey-green water below him and watched as the huge shaggy coated polar bears lunged fiercely in and out of the icy water.

People threw them tit bits and children squealed in delight when the bears lunged for the treats, small eyes 'black as coal', expressionless, snapping with huge yellow teeth. It was a fantastic show.

Maurice thought about Alice. He knew she did not believe him, about Kathleen just leaving like that. He felt the familiar resentment rising up once more when he thought of all the time and secrets his wife must have shared with a complete stranger.

Angrily, he opened his bag and grabbing a handful threw a few chunks into the murky water below him. The bears went wild, jumping up with huge hungry mouths and white shaggy coats as he continued to shower them with the contents of his bag. In and out of the freezing water they plunged. How dare she neglect him! How dare she!

More chunks flew from the bag and hit the surface of the greasy green pond below. In fact, he mused – shaking the now empty bag thoroughly before folding into two and placing it carefully back into his holdall – it might be quite fitting that when the time was right, he arrange for the lovely interfering Alice to join her friend Kathleen, who was now, or at least was slowly, bit by bit joining her only true loves... the polar bears.

The City

Can't believe I'm back here again, after all this time. Nothing much has changed though.

The dirt-lined pavements greet me like broken myriad reflections. City living? Just about, more like city 'surviving'.

Pigeons with their feet rotting serve as a reminder of the filth underfoot, the damp smell of rain mingling with stale cigarette smoke and cheap perfume fills the air around me. Now I know I'm home. I'd forgotten just how depressing this place can be with its chaos and manic crowds.

Moving slowly down from the station pathway in a sort of bizarre Mexican wave, we all pulsate together, spilling snake-like out onto the streets, one constant moving mass of bodies, part of which is me. Jostle, push, every man for himself.

Better than watching street theatre, but without the humour, the destroyed faces of young girls pass by in their clusters, frown lines of disillusionment already beginning to settle in, like ancient maps forming on still virgin-like faces. The odd-ball shouting the odds, the disparate, the desperate, the 'thrown away', all here.

The familiar shuddering starts in my body as the now unwelcomed memories start cascading like the dirty water from the fountains in Piccadilly Gardens, just as icy. No matter how far down you try and bury it, memories of fear and uncertainty are like old familiar friends, ready to step out and assault me from behind my 'new life'. Some stains you cannot rub away no matter how hard you try.

The once magnificent statue of Queen Victoria still dominates the gardens, but even she now sits in a state of distress, not in state. Stoic bronzed face streaked with pigeon shit and red paint, fazing down from frozen eyes on what is left of her 'empire', poor cow.

The gardens were once strewn with flowers I seem to recall; now they are strewn with the broken lives of the drifters, the passers-by, the young boys with their hoods up, hands deep in empty pockets, hiding inside layers of grimy clothing almost indistinguishable from each other. Food wrappers, paper cups, beer cans, newspapers and fag ends. And everyone is nervous, no Garden of Eden here.

In the heart of the city the mobile phone is king. The air crackles with static ringtones, a façade for the desperation that poverty brings, a strange mating call between the lost men, weaving in and amongst the living moving crowds.

Hands thrust out to me, up to me, demanding my attention, money, pity, favours. Bright young men and women appear dotted round the centre of the gardens in bright florescent sweatshirts like exotic blooms amongst the dirt. Clipboards clutched in clean hands with clipped nails, smiles neatly pinned onto fresh faces jump out at me, brilliant guilt-inducing words tumble like a waterfall in a bid to snag me in their charity nets. Campaigning for the poor, launching confidently from their middle class springboards – what the hell could they know about poverty?

Foreign-sounding music filters through the communal gardens from 'suffering' Romanian women, who sit swathed in their bright headscarves, long dirty skirts to the floor, churning out music better suited to the back streets of Paris. Heads bowed subserviently but eyes sharp as eagles watching for pennies to be thrown into grimy tin pots at their feet, sticky hands of their infants just visible from behind the skirts, poor little bastards. The music of the 'dammed' churns on and on.

There is an exceptionally tall tower block in the centre of the city, I know it well. Each time I visit I half expect it to have been demolished. Grey walls concreted and stained with the damp, it rises up floor upon floor and dominates the skyline. On the eleventh floor there is a little battered red door and behind the door I expect to find my 'baby' brother, Marc.

There are about twelve years and three continents between us. No doubt, he is curled up on the sofa, blankets round his shoulders, books in lap. Marc has that soft round face with baby like features that you find on some teenagers and he never seems to change much. His nails are bitten right down to the quick and his blue eyes are fixed in a stare on the text book open in his lap. God he looks so tired. The faint strain of the Romanian women playing their mournful tunes can just be heard up here as we sit together now, 'catching up', drinking mugs of tea, desperately trying not to fill in the silence between us. He is the only 'family' I have left. As for our mother, wherever she is, I'm not sure she deserves anything from either of us.

There is a nightclub called Rafferty's Place in the heart of the northern quarter of the city. It has a terrible reputation for trouble, seems in fact to thrive on it. It's regularly packed to the gills on a Friday. The beer is cheap, so are the women who serve it. I might grab a quick beer in there before heading back to Marc with our fish n chips tea, for old times' sake. You walk through the door and you smell a nasty mixture of stale hops, perfume and sweat. In a far corner of the dingy bar sits a washed up blond, half slumped over the remains of a large gin and tonic. She reminds me, fleetingly, of someone. Just a vague recollection.

Despite her age she still has a soft face, but her shoes and clothes are almost threadbare and her arms are too thin and covered in mottled bruises. She has a short skirt and skimpy top and the tops of her legs are exposed as she shuffles them around under the table in the dark corner. Everyone seems to know her from quick dismissive glances. She looks as if she is daydreaming or maybe just dazed, one grubby hand propping up her face, the other flicking cigarette smoke absently towards a tiny tin foil ashtray in front of her. She looks as if she is trying to remember something important, but it's too painful to linger there for long. So, she turns her face downwards to the gin her hand rests on; her constant friend, her anaesthetic, life saver, lover comfort and joy.

In order to continue this wonderful relationship she needs money so she turns her head towards a large group of workmen standing in a circle in a corner of the pub, pints in hands, suntanned arms exposed along with tattoos, broad backs and thick work boots. What she might call "real men". She momentarily catches one of them with a cheeky raised eyebrow and just as quickly shrinks back, visibly stung under the hard faced detached stare of his eyes. "Been there done that" comes to mind.

The distance between Marc's flat and Rafferty's is hardly worth mentioning, but way up there in the clouds where he lives nothing exists outside of it. Introspective, a 'loner' he spends all his time studying these days, economics; makes me smile whenever I think of it. He who had absolutely nothing as a child, learning all about money – good for Marc. With a long term goal to get out of poverty he has completed his first year and is heading for year two as a Postgraduate. He will heal with his success, I know it.

Our mother. Our very own gin-imbibing whore. She always smelled bad. She is still never far behind me but I think, I hope that Marc was too young to remember everything that happened to us, to him. The splintering china of the mugs she threw against the wall, the torn clothes, and the doors slamming. The desperation and unfulfilled expression always in her eyes when she looked at us, never ever 'a good day' for her.

I had to get out; I had to take myself far away from her before I took her away, somewhere, permanently. I left him behind, had too; Marc was nine. Where could we have gone? That was the first emotional continent I put between him and I; he begged me to take him with me but I just couldn't. So in effect I left him to cope with it, with her, on his own. He never talks about her, just holds her behind his blue eyes, eyes that look just like hers did, bearing silent witness to what they have seen.

Still, now I have seen that he is alive and kicking against the system, working towards finding something better for himself, I will leave with my sense of duty intact. I think I may just stay away from now on, there is no warmth from him to me, just a cold and distant indifference that speaks louder than any words can, he will never forgive me for leaving him behind. But at least he has learned to survive and the fact that he now relies on no one but himself, means I can rest a little easier.

Whistles, shouts and splashing kids with their high squealing voices run in and out of the water fountains around the gardens as I make for the station once more. One last glance back, the scene almost looks biblical, shrouded women, sandaled feet, bearded eyes raised to heaven, thronging towards a promised land that will never materialise.

Competition

That's what it amounted to. He had competition! *His* Jackie, round at their house so regularly.

What did the man think he was going to gain? Gain? He wasn't going to gain anything; in fact he would lose something if it carried on much longer. Jackie always coming home all glowing from the flattery. He knew every inch of his wife's skin, how it moved, how it reacted when she was given a compliment.

She would make out it had all been rather tiresome again and that she only went round to Tom and Lizzie's because she felt sorry for the girl – married to such a prat. He had noticed the way her mouth curled up at the edges ever so slightly whenever he asked her about Lizzie, as if she didn't really want to talk about her – probably too busy dreaming about Lizzie's husband, thought Gregg bitterly!

The last time she had been invited round he had gone with her and, although Lizzie spent most of the time fawning over his wife, (irritating but no big deal; after all Jackie was gorgeous) he felt it was all being staged because he was there. Tom didn't even look at Jackie most of the evening; very suspicious. Jackie always said it was Tom who asked her round to visit them, but that didn't make sense either, too obvious. Something was up and Gregg felt more and more angry about the situation.

He had no choice, he concluded; he would have to 'catch them at it' somehow. He began to set the scene and felt it best done on home turf. He would catch out his cheating wife and so-called good neighbour and that would be an end to it. He would not be treated like a fool!

Two weeks later Tom arrived at the house, bottle of wine under his arm, his other arm wrapped around his mousy wife. Greetings exchanged and drinks poured, Lizzie snuggled into the sofa next to Jackie, a long piece of her hair in her tiny hands, pouring fourth compliments on the colour and the style and oh how she wished her own hair wasn't so dull. Tom, in the meantime, had taken up position next to the fireplace, drink in manly hand and in deep conversation about his latest car. Boring, thought Gregg, just like the man himself. What did Jackie possibly see in him?

She had been flushed as and excited as a school girl with a naughty secret recently, on returning from a visit to their house. They must be being very careful about it all, what with mousy wife clinging like a limpet to Jackie's side most of the time. Gregg knew he would have to get them together and out of sight, somehow.

He took the opportunity of refreshing everyone's drinks and asked Jackie to get some more ice from the freezer in the back room past the kitchen. She dutifully went to fetch some and that is when Gregg asked Tom to go and get another bottle of white out of the fridge for them all. It worked beautifully and both parties were absent for a good few minutes before Gregg charged through the small kitchen and into the back room, fully expecting to see the guilty pair in a hot embrace, only to see his lovely wife chatting brightly to their nerd neighbour about some decorating she was thinking of having done to the back bedroom. Their bodies were miles apart, though Tom's eyes were definitely straying from his wife's face – that much was evident. Tom made an excuse for getting more crisps out and marched back to the mousy one perched on the sofa, who interestingly sat staring at the doorframe her husband had just gone through!

Gregg felt almost cheated, so certain had he been of their infidelity. He also suddenly felt rather foolish and sorry for what he had tried to do. Later he stood in the kitchen with Tom and offered him some ice for his drink, smiling at the man and trying his best to be nice to him, before turning round and leading the way back into the front room, where Jackie had gone before him.

There on the sofa were the two women, hands clasped, lips firmly planted on faces in a snatched loving and terribly guilty embrace...

Mirror

They sit in silence together inside the car, within the park grounds, and look out towards the lake. She turns her head slightly to watch his face, eyes lost somewhere in time – in other memories of the lake – before her, and she can feel the partition in his heart opening up again.

The rain falls with persistence onto the car roof, huge soft heavy blobs like giant's tears, and the car moans a little in protest. Then he returns to her, to this day, the here and now and she is grateful. She asks him to come outside with her – sod the rain! They could walk right around the lake. She knows he wants to.

With a single look into her eyes, this precious man pads out the spaces in her heart that were previously empty. His hands are beautifully warm and he never wears gloves. She squeezes his hand tightly as they set off across the sodden ground. Together now, they will come through anything that life gives them to deal with; they are a team and love is the glue that binds them. She wants this man, she cannot do anything else but love this man.

When he turns to look at her mid-sentence and he frowns with the sincerity of his words, she frowns too. When he is in pain she winces for him. It is indeed a sometimes-strange but definitely privileged place that they are sharing together in this life, like conjoined twins. They feel for each other. The rain falls steadily on them now and the light is grey with the veil of the rain, but the lights in her eyes dance as she looks at his hand covering hers. Safe, loved, here – now.

The rain continues to weep into the lake and the water rises, turning the pond muddy and soup-like. It falls on their heads from the heavens like a silent baptism, but his warm hand over hers is all the protection she needs.

The lake is fringed with old bent trees that stand together like clusters of old friends. The silent mirrored projection of its heart must have witnessed countless lovers strolling under the moonlight, children playing with stones, sunny days and icy nights. Full and secretive, without a voice, this most experienced master of mime sits silently, conveying all that it knows.

At the water's edge they see a few children kitted out in raincoats and bright shiny boots, but the lake is more or less theirs now. He tells her of the children that played by the lake before, of when they were 'spilled out' into the world, into his life, the shock, the beauty. He says it was like the world turning on its axis, the heavens pouring all their stars down onto him, a lesson in humility – a message down the years and centuries from the very beginning of life, the only gift worth having.

He told her he had won the lottery and then it had all been taken away from him again. Just like that. Gone. Left in a dream state of disbelief, doubting every memory, every experience, doubting they had even existed. He said, in the early days, after the disaster the only way he could bear it was to close his eyes and conjure up his children's faces, planting kisses all around their images. She, like the lake, began to mirror this tragedy as she had experienced, but survived, the near death of herself and her child in a major road accident some years before.

She reflected on their mutual friend and there was shared grief, huge grief. Yet her feelings for this complete stranger had stirred her heart with a kind of childish excitement, the tingle of hope that comes with a good feeling. It was as if her heart was pushing through from the back of her sadness, vying for attention with those primary emotions. This was not comfortable but she managed to suppress all of this before leaving abruptly, though tears flooded her eyes. He remained distant and silent.

But now here she was this day, and out of all those ghosts surrounding him he had found a way back into the light. He saw only her, he said. Pulling someone back up to life on strands of hope and glimpses of what could be, back into the real world and out of the depths of the well, isn't an easy task. Not only do you risk failing, you risk succeeding. The prize must be seen to have been worth it or else one might as well live with the certainty of pain.

It was as if in our frailties our strengths lie, though sleeping. But like a song in her head that just kept on repeating itself, he had seeped into her consciousness until he was occupying more of her than she was of herself. She would yield to him. He was worth all the risks.

The rain has eased a little and their walk continues in silence. They are almost at the end, a complete circle. The air is damp but fresh and sweet with the springtime promise of new life. They head back towards the car, hand in hand, ready to tackle whatever the next day brings. Somewhere in the bowels of the earth is the dark hopeless space he once occupied. It remains without an occupant these days – mostly – and she knows that space will slowly crumble and fill up until no trace can ever be found.

They drive back, splashing along the puddled road towards the entrance to the park. There are thin ribbons of blue sky peeping out from under the dark clouds and the rain has eased. One last look at the lake, shimmering silently and looking much smaller in the background now, making them realise that everything is relevant and everything is now. There is only now.

The rain has stopped completely and the air is fresh, new once more.

They met at a funeral.

Dream Girl

To his utter relief, she was there again. With her beautiful black hair cascading down her shoulders and large almost almond shaped eyes, she was truly mesmerising. Talk about the perfect woman, thought Daniel, she had just about everything a man could want. Cupping his thin hands to the window he peered in again, more than aware that he was openly staring at her now, but still somehow unable to stop himself. But it wasn't as if she was making any objection about it and, after all, isn't that what models were all about? To be looked at? Although the other women around her on the opposite side of the glass didn't seem too pleased. The old bat with the tight bun on top of her head gave him a look like thunder, in an attempt to shoo him away from the window.

Finally able to tear himself away, Daniel moved reluctantly and slowly away from the shop window craning his neck back as much as he could before she finally disappeared from view. That window had opened up a window in his heart, a whole new world in fact for Daniel. He turned up the collar of his anorak in an attempt to keep the rain out. But, he really couldn't have cared less about getting wet as he hurried along the pavement, back to work, a picture of her lovely face firmly placed inside his head.

Snapping on the hall light in his small flat at the end of a long and distracting day at work, he headed for the kitchen to make himself a hot drink, his mind still fixated... how could he get her all to himself? What must he do? He had only seen her a few times but was already becoming obsessive about her. All those women around her were so protective-looking – probably wishing they were as gorgeous as her, as she was certainly far more beautiful than any of them.

From the first moment, he had seen her she had occupied his head, woken up his sleeping heart and filled him with a longing he had never felt before in his life. Slipping into the cold bed he closed his eyes slowly, bringing them deliberately to a slit through which he could just conjure up the image of her face; like his own private photograph and the last thing in his sights before drifting into a restless sleep. And again, even in his dreams, he saw her – eyes wide and beautiful flowing hair. He knew he must make a plan so that she could be all his.

Slightly built and not exactly what you would call 'good looking', Daniel had never really been that interested in women before now. Preferring instead his computer games or even crosswords to the pub and socialising. What he wanted, he now realised with some feeling of shame, was the element of voyeurism that she afforded him through the thick glass window. That was what he was enjoying so very much. He wanted to be able to look at her like that every minute of every day, if he so chose. A bit like one of his computer games really, behind the glass, accessible but also something that he could control. He had to think of a way or he would surely go mad!

His frustration increasing, Daniel's mood became more and more erratic. Work colleagues began to avoid him. As the 'office geek' he had never been exactly popular at the best of times, but now he seemed to be behaving even more strangely than normal. Everyone knew there was something eating away at him but no one could be bothered to ask him about it; he just wasn't of that much concern to most of them.

Daniel began to really struggle now, fighting down his desire to tear himself away and run back to the high street – to gaze in through the thick plate window at the one thing he wanted more than anything in the whole world. He began to work longer hours, ensuring he was the last one in the office before leaving to cross the road and stare through the departmental stores huge display windows. He wasn't eating and he wasn't sleeping when finally, and in desperation, he hatched his plan.

The office was a buzz of activity on the following Monday morning when Daniel arrived slightly later than normal. He soon established what the fuss was all about. Apparently it was all to do with the smash and grab raid that had taken place across the road at the large department store. It had happened during the night and apparently designer gowns, jewellery and other expensive accessories had been stolen from the store's display window. They said that whoever had carried it out must have known exactly what they were. As Daniel made his way home that night he seemed to be in a much better mood.

He felt his breath become quite shallow in his chest as he turned the key in the door to his small flat. Perhaps... Perhaps it had all been a dream after all. But no, there she stood in the front room, waiting for him to return. Her long dark hair fell in waves below her slender shoulders and her almond eyes sparkled at him. She was wearing the emerald green Armani dress with the silver trim that she had been wearing the first time he had seen her.

Daniel closed the door softly behind him, took off his jacket and stood back a little just inside the doorframe of the living room, admiring the view. He moved gently across the room and slipped both arms right around her. Holding her in a silent embrace, his breath deep and steady, he stood shaking with love for her. After a long, long time he realised how tired he was. Elated, but tired (the last few days had been quite exhausting after all), he gently released his hold on her and lifting her up in his arms carried her with the utmost care across the dimly lit room. He placed her lovingly in the cupboard next to his bed and then slipped quickly in between the cool sheets, a huge satisfied smile playing across his face. He switched off the bedroom light. She was his, at last.

Prisoner

My husband's face across the visitors' table looks surprisingly fresh, unconcerned even, considering he has just been convicted and sentenced to three whole years in jail for fraud. Three years! My husband! A respectable accountant in a seemingly well paid job. I still can't quite digest it all, still feel the absolute raw shock of hearing the sentence passed on him in court that day, as I sat quietly weeping at the back of the public gallery.

I haven't told any of my friends yet, just can't face up to the shame. No doubt it will have to happen. I can't just ignore everyone for the next three years but I am not ready to face the truth myself yet. Still, I remind myself life must carry on and surely he is suffering more than anyone else now?

He told me he did it because he just couldn't stand to keep living the way we had been, that we needed more money and that things had to change, for all our sakes. None of which made any sense to me. Change things? Well he has certainly achieved that. I took this to mean that he wanted to improve the quality of our lives, that he wanted the very best for his family and, because I knew how stressed he had been for such a long time, I understood that.

I love him so I must try to understand what drove him to do this to us all and then I must try to forgive him.

On my second visit, as I sit and wait for him to enter the crowded visitors' room and find me, he appears in the doorway. Our eyes meet momentarily from across the large room as he weaves his way in and out of the tables towards me. His black wavy hair has been trimmed short now, closer to his head, giving his features more credit. He looks, in fact, positively handsome as I sit across from him on the other side of the worn out Formica table, pouring out my grievances; about managing the house alone, about Katy's first tooth coming through, my mother's constant nagging me to divorce him. I tried at first fobbing her off with a story about him working away from home for a while up at the head office in Glasgow. But she always did know when I was lying and of course the tears eventually came, along with the truth.

He just watches my face impassively, like someone in a trance and all I can think is he must still be in shock and hasn't come to terms with things yet. On the other hand, neither have I.

Weeks go by and I am still waiting for an apology – for what he has done to us, to our family, to me. I can no longer hold my head up in public, I am avoiding all contact with my friends and there is no money coming in. Even the journey to the prison means taking two buses as it's right on the outskirts of town. Thank god for that small mercy as at least I am unlikely to bump into anyone I know.

On the second bus now on the way to the visitors' hall, I succeed in pushing my anger down as far as it will go, but once in front of him again it surfaces and threatens to rear its ugly head. I find myself steering the conversation towards another argument, never quite reaching its full pitch but constantly threatening to. This time it's all just too much. I am worn out as Katy doesn't sleep at night now she is teething, the bills are being left unpaid and I am beginning to feel like a widow.

I cannot hold back my anger any longer as I scream like a mad woman at my husband across the table in the hot crowded room, calling him every name I can think of, face bright red and stinging with long held back tears. All heads turned at me, bleached blonds with tattoos, teenagers and prison warders, all eyes on me, accusatory, as if some invisible rule has been broken. Harry says nothing but I swear he had the beginnings of a smile on his face as he got up abruptly and left me at the table still shouting and crying. I cannot describe how I felt, abandoned mostly and all this played out in front of an audience of complete strangers.

Harry's laid back approach to what has happened to him, and indeed to the sentence itself, had horrified me initially. But I kept on telling myself you don't live with someone for fifteen years and not know them; know that he must be in shock and that one day – probably suddenly on one of these awful enforced visits of mine – he will just break down, come clean about his guilt and actually finally say he is sorry. It didn't happen.

Trying to stay calm I manage to inject a little humour into the next conversation we have. I am quite frankly just grateful now that he has chosen to see me again after what happened on my last visit. I decide to just ignore the outburst too, for the sake of sanity. I tell him about the mundane, the work colleague called Sandra who is so clumsy and how she tripped whilst carrying a tray full of tea and cakes. Looking at his face, if feels a bit like throwing water at a glass surface, the drops just keep dripping down and off, no movement or reaction at all. He attempts a smile but it is hollow and meaningless and leaves me cold. He is clearly not the slightest bit interested in me or anything I have to say.

The bell rings and we are both released from the soulless time we have just spent together, people stand up, chairs scraping the ground in chorus. I bend forward to my kiss goodbye and feel a stab of pain in my heart as he kisses my cheek, not my lips. I leave the visitors hall in a daze, wondering where the hell my husband has gone.

Over the last few months Harry had been working harder than ever, we had Katy and a baby costs a lot of money – but I always felt so proud of him, working late, always offering to go in over the weekends. I missed him not being with us at home, but because I knew he was working for the benefit of us all I respected him for that, was happy to let him do it. What with Katy on my hands and being so tired all the time, it was the least I could do. Even when he became defensive and moody, secretive even, I just put it all down to tiredness. Perhaps, now I am beginning to see that he must have been quite miserable. We both knew that Katy might have been the most difficult thing to cope with.

He had made it clear to me from the start of our relationship that he didn't want any more children – already the father of two teenagers when we first met, it was understandable. But when I begged him to reconsider for the thousandth time, crying myself to sleep over and over, he had finally given in. But it had never been his choice to have a baby. Perhaps, just perhaps, he had begun to resent her presence in our lives more than I had ever realised? I tried to make sense of the random thoughts echoing round my head, but the more I tried to work it out the more confused I became. Surely, we had been happy hadn't we?

Back home, I try to busy myself with baking cakes, cleaning the oven doors with sponge and detergent before setting off to collect Katy from the child-minder. The child-minder! That will have to stop, no money. If that stops, my job at the library stops and we will probably have even less to manage on. I pull myself in sharply and think of my husband, his isolation, lack of privacy and freedoms all gone. I must be grateful.

Oh damn, Harry, damn you. What have you done to me, to Katy? His beautiful little girl who constantly looks for her daddy even though she is not old enough to understand why he suddenly isn't there any more. Katy, whose shoes need replacing and who is about to lose her child-minder all because of him!

On my next visit I notice that he is actually putting on weight. He tells me the food is quite good and that he doesn't have much to do in the day. I feel terribly resentful listening to this, especially when I think of the tight budget that I am now left with, the child-minder gone, the money finally run out. She was so lovely about it, even offering to bridge the gap until finances improved – I was forced to tell her that wasn't likely to happen anytime soon.

Then my job went. No one to mind Katy, impossible for me to work. We are claiming benefits now and looking at my husband, the menu is evidently not as good in my house as it is in prison!

Harry looks remotely smug, sort of once removed from me, his wife, and my complaints and I can feel the tears begin to well up behind my tired eyes. I have to take coupons to the supermarket to get free bread and milk; we walk miles out of the way to find the best value shops these days, no wonder I am so slim. I can no longer get out to the swimming pool in the evenings, can't even afford a babysitter now. My house is my prison it seems.

On the bus journey home, in between getting off the first bus and waiting to catch the second, I find myself quite alone; Katy is with the next door neighbour. Standing in the darkened bus shelter next to an open field with no one around for miles, I open my mouth and allow myself to just scream and scream until the tears pour down my face and the terrible tension in my exhausted body subsides. I wipe my face as best I can as I glimpse the approaching bus in the far distance.

I catch my eyes in the bathroom mirror. I have about me now the look of someone haunted. Sallow complexion, tired, hurt eyes. As I stand in the tiny bathroom, I feel truly trapped, in a dead end. In an effort to fight off my demons I get a chair and climb onto it, to reach up to the hatch that leads to the attic. I will sort out the attic; that should knock the wind out of me.

Much later, still sitting amongst piles of dust and old cardboard boxes, discarded lamp stands and the fold down Christmas tree that Harry hated so much, I come across a small leather holdall. It's crammed full of letters, documents and accounts of some sort. I cannot make head nor tale of it but amongst the rows and rows of figures I see he has written what looks like a note to someone else.

It starts with "I think I have found a solution, my love". It's definitely Harry's writing. A solution to what? And if it's to me then why didn't he give me the note? I feel distinctly uncomfortable. What did he mean? A solution? To what? That was all there was, nothing else to explain the words nothing to go on. I shut the book and decided that my over active imagination is probably trying to get the better of me.

However, when I think of my husband's now quite rotund and even contented features that tell me he has simply withdrawn from his responsibilities, I begin to realise, truly for the first time, just who has become the prisoner.

The Dropped Baby

Christ, he was hot. Sweat kept dripping down the back of his thick muscled neck and prickling his hairline.

Something about the heat enables us to open our usually more confined selves, the borders of possibility expand as the heat opens us up to greater self-awareness and with that comes clarity. Something about the sun enables us to locate spaces inside ourselves that we don't usually have access to, those deep hidden crevices where we put all our anger and sorrow, shining its light deep down in the very lining of us. All those thoughts and feelings buried in the belief they would not need to be accessed again.

Christ, he was hot and angry now, angry most days but today *really* angry. He was surely *the* only person in the world suffering today, there simply was no room for *anyone else* and he felt aggrieved and irritable.

The hot tarmac began plucking at the soles of his boots as he marched along the narrow pavement before crossing the main road and into the shopping mall. Sudden blasts of icy air began hitting his skin as he crossed the entrance into air conditioning heaven.

This felt better but he still felt angry and irritable, cross with God even, cursing the arms and legs of the child that brushed past him, the red mist descending. *Better watch out*, the familiar voice inside his head said. Lost it all on the gee gees, over ten thousand pounds and there *she* was, clear in his mind's eye, having got what *she* wanted from him, sitting pretty in her Castle with her Knight.

He had always known what the deal was, just hadn't anticipated how he would feel about the end result. Now that he had nothing and she had got everything she had ever wanted, a part of *him*, forever, he was feeling very angry.

He had had to glean information about the baby from Maggie, her cleaner of all people, and that had cost him a few doubles. Maggie had eventually told him that Laura had had a baby girl and then asked him why he had been so interested.

Late summer sun shone consistently through the large sashcord windows, down onto the wooden floorboards, creating golden warmth that seemed to hover above the floor. Laura leant back against a dozen small soft cushions and gazed at the long boughs of the willow tree, as they danced rhythmically up and down on the other side of the windows.

She put a neatly manicured hand on the rather large solid stomach in front of her and felt a good strong kick from the baby inside. Not long now, she thought, thank God.

It hadn't been easy for Laura, this pregnancy, having to bend to someone else's will even though in this case it was for something she had agreed to and thought she wanted. But in truth, it was not part of her natural makeup. Now, she was just about at the end of her patience with it all. The baby moved again under her hand, as if in response to her thoughts. Of course she wanted the 'end result' she had just resented the process and now she just wanted her body back.

Having shared an extremely indulgent and intimate twelve years with her husband, Thom, and having realised he would never be able to father a child, Laura had carried out what she had seen as the only option open to her. She had chosen, physically, very similar to Thom – beautifully put together, someone strong. She had been lucky the first time. It had been a small price to pay.

Of course she had known the shift in priorities was bound to have an effect – morning sickness doesn't exactly go with romantic weekends away – but it alarmed her somewhat, just how angry being so limited had made her feel.

It was time to prepare the evening meal, the effort of standing up made her gasp a little...

Intense light above dazzled her eyes as she lay on her back on the rapidly moving trolley. Shouts punched the air from faraway places off the corridor. Someone was talking about her from above – a fresh faced young nurse kept looking down at her and telling her that she was 'doing very well' and to 'keep taking those deep breaths'. Laura would have happily slapped her face had she been able to concentrate on anything other than the pain – and where was her husband?

Looking back, baby Millie had made quite a dramatic entrance into the world. Laura had been about to test the vegetables still roasting in the oven, and had not been expecting the horrendous pain of sudden onset labour. As she watched helplessly, the water streamed down her legs onto the black and white tiles of the kitchen floor.

Millie lay on her back, all soft, out-of-focus eyes and wet mouth. Perfectly formed limbs moving rhythmically to the beating of her heart. She's perfect, thought Laura as she observed her tiny daughter. She can do no wrong. Laura was very tired, quite aware of her sarcasm but unable to control it.

Getting up to feed Millie in the middle of the night was now more of an ordeal than anything else, she felt sore most of the time and increasingly resentful. One hand resting on her stomach, empty now of its burden, she realised this was not the way she had imagined things would be. She would put Millie onto a bottle, despite Thom's protestations – *he* didn't have to feed her all the time.

Mum and Dad had adored their first granddaughter, naturally. But when her mother suggested that she 'try and diet sooner rather than later, darling, especially being an older mum', followed by an acerbic 'got to get that fabulous figure back', it left her face burning indignantly, the resentment rising up a few more notches.

Laura looked wearily around the expensively furnished nursery, all the latest toys and stuffed animals, baby mats, a hand carved rocking horse. She had thought her part in things would have been easier by now; she had carried the baby after all. She turned away from the nursery and made her way down the wide staircase and towards the sound of laughter coming from the kitchen, Thom 'holding court' with her parents and close friends yet again, no doubt. Still she could murder a glass of wine and as she wouldn't be breast feeding any more...

Half way through her third glass of chilled Chablis it was fairly obvious Laura was getting drunk. She was vaguely aware of her mother's disapproving face, hovering somewhere over her husband's shoulder, though she also knew her mother wouldn't dare show her up in front of them all – not if she valued contact with her precious granddaughter.

The kitchen buzzed with chatter, mostly coming from two work colleagues from Thom's office who Laura actually hardly knew – all slender arms and legs and neatly pinned hair. Even the dangling earrings on one of them annoyed Laura beyond belief. *She* wouldn't be wearing earrings like that for a long time, not with Millie trying to grasp at them.

Laura disliked the way she was feeling about both her mother and her daughter but she just couldn't bring herself out of it. She made an excuse about getting tea ready and left them all to it, just before her husband was about to steer her away into another room and ask what the hell the matter was.

It happened when Millie was almost six weeks old. Everyone was shocked but of course at the same time deeply sympathetic. After all, no one in their right mind would do something like that on purpose, would they?

Laura's parents, her younger sister and her partner, several neighbours and two elderly aunties were all spread around the sitting room, wine and canapés in hands, admiring the new baby, raising their glasses in toasts to the resplendent pink-clad infant. Wasn't she well behaved? Isn't she adorable, little doll…

Laura, on her third glass of wine, sat perched on the edge of the sofa, holding in her stomach, fixed smile in place, when she suddenly felt the whole room closing in on her. The feeling of being out of control escalated – this was meant to be *her* day, *her* moment to shine, as well as her baby's!

Chattering faces, bright colours, heat of the sun through the window, the effects of the wine… Without warning she lunged towards her sister, Sarah, who was holding Millie securely on her lap with two firm hands and grabbed at the baby, smiling widely as she did so. Plucking her daughter out of her sister's firm grip resulted in both women losing hold of the tiny bundle and Millie went crashing to the floor like a deadweight. The silence was palpable.

With sly eyes and trembling lips, Laura slid to the floor to retrieve the stunned baby who, making no noise whatsoever, lay glassy-eyed on her back on the floor. The piercing wail from the baby broke the silence from the horrified audience, bringing with it a cascade of reactions. Everyone was fussing around the floor where the baby fell or trying to stroke Laura's back in reassurance, collectively relieved that the baby was going to be all right.

The 'incident' wasn't talked about again, at least not in public. It became something everyone preferred to forget or at worst discuss furtively behind their own front doors. "All that privilege and no mothering skills whatsoever", or "The stupid cow, she was always wanting attention".

Undertones of disturbance began to ripple through Laura's marriage to Thom, the viciousness with which she had tried to snatch back her daughter, the wine. Thom wouldn't let this one go without a fight. And fight they did, constantly about the baby and her unfit state.

She felt desperately angry and sad that Thom was taking the baby's side and not hers, her mind moving further into black places filled with paranoia and delusion.

She only agreed to counselling when he threatened to take the baby over to her mother's house to stay. The thought of her bloody mother getting any sort of control made Laura feel sick – hadn't she had enough control over her, Laura, as a small child?

Thom was in Holland on business, the first time he saw fit to leave Laura alone with the baby since the 'incident'. Consequently, he had left her with strict instructions that she must phone him regularly and that if she felt the slightest bit 'wobbly' then he would return immediately.

It was on the first night of being alone that Laura moved silently into the nursery and stared towards the source of all her troubles. She had thought about it long and hard and had finally reached a conclusion. There was only room for one female in her household. Laura moved unsteadily towards the cot.

The Journey

Mary watched her feet as she slowly walked on towards the town. She wore her 'respectable' brown leather walking shoes as she paced painfully forward; one, the other; one, the other, carrying her stiff body onwards. Her mother had drummed it into her from an early age, "If you want to be respected you wear respectable shoes, Mary." But today she didn't feel at all robust and her 'respectable shoes' were hurting her feet.

In fact she felt as if her heart might just break into a thousand little pieces through the dismal pain she was feeling. What was the matter with her today? All right, she had arthritis but why did it seem to be so very bad today?

It occurred to her then that she had suddenly become very old and alone, probably not needed by anybody anymore. And, at that moment, she felt her very spirit lying inside her, panting and wide-eyed like a frightened child trying desperately to escape.

Perhaps, she thought, I have – what was it called? – dementia? You do hear about people of my age going funny with it, she mused as she continued to walk slowly and painfully on towards the town.

A single tear found its way out of her eye as a group of rowdy teenagers, with their whole lives in front of them and all the arrogance of youth, came bustling towards her on the narrow pavement. Her tight grey curls itched her head and her thin skin seemed to shun even the warmth of the sun's rays today. Deep in her heart she cried out loud to be free and young like them once more, to escape this 'cage' that she had become.

She passed an old man who appeared very confused and as they passed on the pavement he attempted to meet her eyes. She felt herself recoil slightly, as if by acknowledging them she would also be acknowledging herself in them.

Hurrying along as best she could she felt the oh-so-familiar shooting pains in her arthritic hip as her feet padded painfully forward in their respectable shoes, on towards the town that she must surely reach soon.

She looked across the street at a young man, all muscled and suntanned and, to her immense shame, suddenly wanted to reach out and touch him, to touch his youth to try and transport herself back to her own. Shaking her head gently from side to side, she continued on her way towards the town that seemed to her to be so very much further away today.

And then, suddenly in her mind's eye, she was once again lying on that large bed in the heat of the afternoon, Hugo by her side sleeping peacefully, one large arm wrapped protectively across her body. She shuddered violently at the forgotten delight of that memory, a memory she realised now that was over sixty years old. That was the night before he went off to fight for his country, she recalled, sighing deeply, her soft grey head shaking with the memory.

That was the last time she ever saw her dear Hugo. She would have married him, had he come back to her from the war but he never did return, and so she never married, throwing herself instead into a long career in teaching.

She tutted to herself now. What was she doing? Feeling this way now, after all these years had passed. She was not given to losing control of her emotions easily. But she was aware that the recent death of her only brother was probably the reason behind all these silly thoughts. After all, who was there left for her to relate to now, or be with or even visit?

Why am I still here? What is the point in anything any more? she thought as she felt her feet leave the pavement and rise slowly into the air. The higher she rose, the smaller the people on the ground became and she felt the years dropping away from her, felt her limbs becoming looser, free from the pain and then... she saw him. Her dear Hugo, waving to her from above, just smiling and waving at her, his strong arms wide open and encouraging, waiting for her and she knew then that everything was going to be all right.

The crowd around the old lady thinned out to make room for the ambulance men – she lay very still across the pavement, her nice respectable shoes had come off her feet – free at last.

Last Dance

He was forever hopeful, was Geoff, thought Martine as she watched people arriving at the club from her seat at the side of the ballroom. Eyes always lit up like lanterns, face carefully arranged in a welcoming smile, hope in his heart – for what, she now wondered – always for something new, that's what motivated him, she thought. Not for him, the beauty of stability – he was much more attracted by, well, by beauty itself really and the endless possibilities that all those lovely women could offer him.

Martine was just short of retirement from the travel agents she had worked for all her life, approaching her sixties and lonely, and so it felt as though all her Christmases had come at once when Geoffrey Salmon first took her proudly on his arm and out onto the dance floor.

Looking back, she thought now, she had probably been his last piece of 'sanity'. After a string of temporary 'arrangements' they had come together and something wonderful began to happen for them both. Martine honestly thought that it would go on forever.

However, since dumping her, so unceremoniously, he just hadn't looked the same – he looked more manic somehow, intense even, fighting off the impending years obviously took all his time up. Everyone had noted the hair dye and fake tan. Along with the rest of the group – it had made her cringe really and feel grateful that at least whilst he'd been with her, he hadn't felt the need to dress like that.

Geoff had made Martine feel like a young girl again, that first time those strong hands held her waist as he guided her firmly round the dance hall floor, his eyes locked into hers. He was good in bed too. No doubt all those years of dancing had kept his body well-toned and he was certainly enthusiastic! It lasted almost two years between them but she had honestly thought that 'he was the one'; that at the grand age of sixty-two she had been lucky enough to find true love again.

She had enjoyed a happy marriage with Tony for almost twenty years before he left her for a neighbour and she honestly never thought she would find happiness with another man ever again. So it really did break her heart when Geoff took her to their 'favourite restaurant' – for what she had thought would have been a lovely meal out together – and then, before they had even ordered their meals, announced it was over between them, that he was sorry.

When she asked him, tearfully what she had done wrong, he had replied, "Nothing, Martine I just don't feel the way I used to about you".

She left him sitting at the little table, with his face closed off from her, her new and unknown future ahead of her. That was, what... Six months ago now.

I must admit, he did earn my astonished admiration, if only for his cheek, thought Martine, when some two weeks after we split up, two new women joined our dancing group, mother and daughter evidently.

The daughter, Julia, being somewhere in her late thirties, had a pretty face framed with long flowing brown hair and a peaches and cream sort of complexion. The mother, Audrey, was a somewhat more worn down version of her daughter. He was openly admiring of Julia from the start, the smile, the charm, oozing out of every pore. I remember it well.

He began to turn up to classes in tighter trousers, the beginnings of a pot belly protruding slightly from a tight silk cummerbund, absurd really. He almost completely ignored her mother, which was, I thought, a very immature thing to do. But this behaviour obviously reflected his goal, another conquest with no intention of considering the long term. It hurt, though, having to watch him making advances on someone else, younger and prettier than me.

The 'long term' had occurred to me, lying on my bed after he had left me one evening, my imagination seeing us somewhere in a rosy glowing future, together. We liked the same things, didn't we? Always a good place to start. I still remember the feeling of pure joy and tingling anticipation that filled me as I allowed my mind to wander freely down that imaginary path.

On reflection now, what a silly woman I must be! I had completely ignored the warning glances of the other women in the group when Geoff had made it obvious to them all that he was 'with me'. I had shut my ears to the gossip that he was a womaniser and I was just the next 'in a very long line'. Nothing more, nothing less.

The Christmas Dance was looming when things all came to a head. Everyone at our club was excited and looking forward to the event. We traditionally made a huge effort with our costumes as rival clubs were always invited and, although not official, there was fierce competition! I chose to wear a bright yellow number this year, partly because I was not in the mood to play the wallflower and partly because I knew Geoff hated the colour yellow!

Besides I thought I could wear it well considering my quite substantial weight loss. I thought I looked pretty damn good as I stood before my bedroom mirror, the night of the dance. My arms looked shapely and firm, bust all organised tightly under the straps of black organza that lined the bodice and the waist of my outfit. Hair okay, make up perfect. Not bad at all! Perhaps, my foolish heart fluttered, he might even notice me tonight.

Sweeping that last rather self-defeating thought away as quickly as possible, I placed my cape around my shoulders, switched off the lights and made my way into the cool evening and my waiting taxi. I felt surprisingly calm and self-possessed as I made my late entrance, planned deliberately to bring maximum attention as I knew Lorna and Margery would be waiting anxiously to see what I was wearing and to show their own outfits off.

As I entered the ballroom doorway, I knew something was wrong. Why wasn't the band playing? Where was everyone? Not a sequin in sight as I continued along the entrance hall and turned right into the huge ballroom itself. In the far corner I could see a huddle of women, all organza and shimmering feathers as they jostled and moved around whatever was happening down on the floor. Lifting the hem of my dress I made a quick dash across the parquet floor in order to gain a better view. What on earth was going on?

Pushing aside a handful of gowns and shimmer I finally managed to get a view into the circle. The young woman who had taken Geoff's fancy – Julia – was down on her knees, bent right over him, her scarlet painted mouth literally clamped onto his as he lay motionless on his back on the floor. Then I noticed his colour, or rather lack of it – she was trying to revive him!

The bar, all lit up with miniature fairy lights and strands of tinsel, stood eerily empty at the other end of the hall as I slowly approached it, the young waiter behind it looking awkward with no one to serve. Cold gin and tonic stung the back of my throat as I knocked it back. The ice was so cold, a single tear escaped from my eye and dropped soundlessly into my lap. Strange how someone can break your heart more than once.

The Nuisance

It was something and nothing. It had started a few weeks before when Jen had happened to glance up and look out of the window, across to the multi-storey car park facing the building.

That's when she first saw it; a small face, about three or four inches across and made of what looked like some sort of metal. It was barely discernable really but she saw it and she clearly saw that it was, or appeared to be, looking straight back at her.

It obviously wasn't a real face – she wasn't an idiot – but somehow someone had put it there right on the top floor of the car park exactly level with her floor, in fact, her window. And now that she had seen it, she just couldn't stop looking out at it.

It had no expression, just the features any face would have, eyes, a mouth and a nose. Even from behind her PC monitor and workstation there was no hiding from it. She tried to move her computer round and adjusted the angle of her chair, but still it stood firmly in the corner of her vision. What had started off amusing her had now begun to seriously irritate her.

She knew she was being irrational, and that it really didn't matter. It was just a stupid inanimate object and she must press on with her reports or she would be in trouble with her line manager again.

But each day the compulsion to raise her eyes to the window and snatch a look at the face overpowered her and won. She flicked her eyes up at it and then down to her work again, more and more until, sometimes, she had to just get up and walk away from her desk to calm down. This was ridiculous, she told herself almost daily now, she was behaving like a lunatic. But still the 'nuisance' stood there, perfectly still, grinning mechanically in the far distance.

Whenever she took a phone call her eyes flicked over to its face, whenever she had a visitor to her desk she tried to block her view to the window with one hand. She began to feel as if she were being watched, her privacy invaded. She began to feel that the face was laughing at her.

She couldn't tell anyone about it, she just couldn't – they would dismiss it out of hand, call her a drama queen or worse. No, she wasn't going there. She would have to try and do something about it herself, she had to or else she would surely go mad.

Jen knew all the building attendants well and so one evening, after a particularly stressful day, she decided to take things into her own hands. She went along to their little office on the ground floor and chatted amiably to a couple of the porters before asking about a car parking space in the multi-storey – was there a waiting list, how much did it cost?

She was half thinking of driving into work and wondered if there would be the chance of a space for her car? She ended it all with a request to have a quick look round the place, see for herself?

This suggestion was taken with a pinch of amusement from the porters. But they said they didn't see why not and when Albert offered to go across there with her, his big bunch of keys jangling from a thick belt, she jumped at the chance. Albert opened the large metal doors and they got into the lift. Jen said she wanted to go to the top floor, made a joke about wanting to see her office, which would be just in line from up there. They got out of the lift and stepped out into the cool air of the rooftop space.

Jen went to the place she knew the 'nuisance' should be but saw nothing, checking all along the metal barrier she simply could not find anything other than the smooth steel of the protective barriers! She didn't understand at all. It must have fallen off or been taken off! She felt the hint of a smile curling her lips slightly. She didn't actually care how this had come about, she was just glad that it had. Albert stood a few feet away, watching her distractedly before finally shouting to ask if she had seen enough.

"Oh yes," she said. She had just wanted to see the view – and asked him to please let her know when the next space became available. Albert promised he would.

Jen went straight home, happy, rather tired but sure now that she would no longer be troubled by the stupid face looking at her every day and ruining her concentration! She ran a hot bath, watched rubbish TV for an hour, then headed off for an early night.

As she entered the building the next morning she felt completely different knowing the 'nuisance' was no more had really changed her mood. She took the lift to the fourth floor then took the steps two by two up the last floor just for fun. She had been settled into her chair for a few seconds at most, one hand on the computer ready to switch on when something caught her eye.

It was back. The face. It was back. What the? She stood up and went straight to the window, pressing her nose against it so she could see it quite clearly. Someone had put the metal face back again. Someone was out to tease her, she felt sure about that now. But who and why? It couldn't have been Albert – far too disinterested and slow. She calmed her breathing down and resolved to try not to even glance at the window for the rest of the day. Someone – whoever that was – had a rather peculiar sense of humour but she wasn't going to let it upset her. She flicked her eyes up once at the end of the day – it was still there.

Jen went quietly and quickly into the porters' office. No one around later in the evenings. She quickly took the spare master key to the multi-storey car park from its hook inside the large metal box and left as quietly as she had come in.

Once on the roof of the car park she marched straight towards the barrier in the semi light but could see nothing. No metal face once again, just the smooth metal barriers as before. She couldn't even see any marks or scratches where someone might even have attached the bloody thing. Highly puzzled now – she had fully expected to see it this time – she turned to leave.

She didn't know where she was for quite a few minutes when she finally came round. The first face she saw reminded her a little of the 'nuisance', a sort of half formed blurred face staring down at her. Her mother's familiar features finally came into focus and she breathed a sigh of relief.

Sudden flashes of memory came to her then, a vague recollection of being on the car park roof – then tumbling through the air, falling over the barrier in response to the massive blow to the back of her head. They were all talking at her as if she was an idiot, or something to be pitied, her mother in tears, the doctor looking very concerned. She tried to sit up but got shot through with tremendous pain. She gathered she would be in hospital for quite a while, having broken so many bones. She was lucky to be alive, they said.

Lying painfully back down and closing her bruised eyelids once more, Jen slowly turned her throbbing head towards the window, there in the corner of her vision sat the metal face. This time it looked almost as if it was smiling.

Cheeseplant

The bright morning sunshine slowly filled the neatly painted room, boxes and crates catching its first rays. Susie stretched out her arms from under the woollen blanket and emerged slowly blinking with sleep, shielding her eyes from the brightness in the room.

Surveying the neat little front room, she thought it was almost a shame to have to fill it up as she most surely would, with all her bookcases and lamps, nest of tables and framed photographs. It would shrink the room terribly but that was life, she mused. One day she would be able to afford a much bigger place to live. She ran a sleepy hand through her thick chestnut hair and padded softly, in slippered feet, out into the little hallway.

In an instant, the sleepiness vanished as she visibly jerked her whole body, almost toppling backwards into the front room again as there, towering right over her, stood the tallest cheese plant she had ever seen. It had really startled her. "Surely," she said out loud to it, "you weren't there last night!"

Immediately she felt rather stupid, talking to a bloody plant, and painfully aware of a creeping headache caused by the whole bottle of Prosecco she had managed to consume by herself. But she also felt strangely uneasy because she genuinely did not recall seeing something so big and quite frankly obstructive, sitting in her hallway almost filling it up completely! The last owners of the flat must have just left it there and not bothered to tell her, but she was still quite sure she had gone to bed not the owner of such a monster. Mind you, she knew that with almost a bottle of wine inside her anything was possible! She must have just not thought it was that large last night in the semi darkness of the porch, and the broken light fitting hadn't helped. In fact, it had all seemed like one huge jumble of odd shapes last night.

Susie stepped gingerly towards it and examined it. Ribbon after ribbon of lush green leaves, thick and rubbery, it seemed to almost reach the ceiling. Feeling slightly angry now, she decided she didn't want it in her new home, blocking the sunlight from her porch. She aimed a kick at its shiny green tub making its branches and leaves all tremble violently. This was all she needed. But the plant could wait; she had other much more urgent things to do this morning. Besides, how the hell was she supposed to move the stupid thing all on her own?

She spent the next few hours unpacking her bits and pieces, unwrapping ornaments and photographs from the layers of newspaper they had been transported in. The sunshine grew even more intense in the little room and, even a room away, she could smell a slightly earthy odour coming down the hall – the plant! She felt irritated all over again, but decided to stop for some much-needed coffee before thinking about how to get it outside. She boiled her nice shiny new kettle and made a huge mug of steaming dark coffee. Sipping the hot liquid she momentarily closed her eyes, but quickly opened them again when she heard a loud cracking thump from the hallway. She felt her heart beating way too fast as she slowly put her coffee down and edged towards the doorway.

The cheese plant lay across the hall. Soil and tiny stones had showered her nice clean carpet and globules of soggy soil sat in pooling clumps all over the floor and walls. Disbelief was soon replaced by sheer rage as she rushed towards the fallen giant, pushing wildly at its trunk, grabbing its huge shiny leaves in an attempt to pull it upright again. She felt the leaves shredding in her hands as she pulled and tugged in vain. Finally exhausted, she plopped down onto the carpet to gather her energy and emotions.

What to do now? The bloody thing had, somehow, fallen right across the hallway effectively blocking her way out. Tears threatened to overpower her as she now realised she had no way of communicating with the outside world. The previous owner had had the landline disconnected and her mobile had been lost on a girls' night out just before she moved in – it was first on her list to be replaced. She slowly backed away from her tormentor.

With the beginnings of a smile starting on her pale face, she flew to the packing box in the corner of the front room and rummaged around in it until she emerged with her large scissors. She would cut her way out! She would hack its branches off, one by one if necessary!

The first few attempts bore little fruit as some of the stems of the plant were as thick as her fingers. But, with gritted teeth and a determination that she had rarely felt before, she started making some progress, cutting and hacking at the stalks and leaves and throwing them behind her in great handfuls. She was only forced to stop when she felt the familiar shooting pains start in her left leg and then travel quickly up to her lower back. Cursing her sciatica, she had no choice but to lie down on a patch of carpet and keep her back as straight as she could manage, given the lack of space.

Looming up above her, the giant plant somehow looked as huge as it had before she had attacked it, as she lifted her eyes up to it from the floor. She tried to move, but couldn't tolerate the shooting pains and lay still and trembling in the shadow of the damaged plant. Everything went black then.

When Susie's parents finally persuaded the police to break down the door, the first thing they saw was a huge damaged cheese plant sprawled out across the porch, literally blocking it. Then, when they finally moved it out of the way enough to gain access to the flat – Susie.

Taken For a Ride

"Went out into the countryside today with Billy, we must have covered more than six miles, just me and Billy. I feel like he has given me a new lease of life."

These last words, written in such a familiar handwriting sent an ice-cold shiver through Ray's heart. He couldn't take it in, couldn't quite believe what he was reading. Blinking back tears he stared at the open diary in his lap.

She had gone over to her mother's earlier in the evening and when he had knocked a pile of reading books off the table next to the chair, it suddenly seemed impossible for him to resist picking up her diary. It had tumbled to the floor and lay there, pages wide open, pinned to the floor like a butterfly, asking to be picked up and read – although he knew he was breaking all their rules.

They had always respected each other's private thoughts; it was something they agreed on. People need their own private spaces but now – now was different, and the rules had all suddenly changed.

He turned his wheelchair round and sat hunched in it for a long time, eyes streaming with tears. It had felt like the end of the world when they told him he was highly unlikely to ever have the use of his legs back, after the accident – but this, this felt even worse. This was his Meg, his wife, his life.

When he had reached for the diary he had half expected to find something written down about him. After all, Meg was only just thirty years old, beautiful, vibrant, her whole life in front of her. She must have felt anger and bitterness about his accident too – not that she had ever said so to his face. She must have needed some private space to express her feelings, let them out.

What he had expected was something along those lines, a way of self-expression for her – not this! Who the hell was Billy? What he didn't expect was another blow to be dealt with such force to his already fragile ego.

Picking up the diary once more, Ray opened it up at the same page. Forcing himself to look at the words he re-read her account of the day out with 'Billy' and continued to read – all about how she knew she shouldn't be nurturing this love she was feeling for Billy but that she felt free and alive again when she had him to herself. She had even written that she knew how much it would hurt Ray if he found out!

Having embarked on a journey from which now there was simply no return, he read on. It appeared from her diary entries that she had been seeing this 'Billy' for some time now, at least a few months anyway. How on earth could she have kept this from him? Purporting to love him, stroking his face, holding his hands, reassuring him of their future together and all the while seeing someone else?

The sound of the front door slamming jolted him out of a dreamlike state and back into the reality that was about to unfold. He looked towards the doorway and there she was, framing it in an instant. "Hello, love, did you miss me?" Beautiful, smiling Megan, blonde hair, peachy skin, blue eyes. How could she?

Staring at his useless legs, he had never felt quite so much pity for himself in his entire life. Meg stood, watching his face closely. Now is the time, he told himself. Now or never.

"Who the hell is Billy?" he shouted at her. There it was, done. Trust broken, nothing left to hide. She had no choice now but to spit it out, tell him when she was leaving him, why she was leaving him... Meg's face portrayed her inner turmoil as she visibly struggled to form her words.

She slumped forward into the room and sat down heavily on the edge of the sofa. "Oh, my darling, my sweet man, I am so sorry. I know I have been selfish, beyond words, especially after your accident... I didn't tell you because I didn't want to upset you – I mean you won't ever ride again and I just thought you would never want me to again either, not after your back, not..."

"Just tell me!" he shrieked. The agony of this delaying tactic was just too much for him to listen to.

"It's true!" Meg burst back at him. "Billy is Dianne's you know, not mine, I just borrow him now and then. I ride him out across the fields at the back when you want a quiet day or when you are sleeping."

Ray's face opened up like a flower, eyes wide in disbelief. "A horse? A bloody horse?"

He started to laugh then, almost hysterical with relief and as he laughed, Meg began to realise what her diary entries must have looked like to her poor husband and she started to laugh along with him.

"Oh, my darling Meg, my sweet love, it's only a silly horse, and you have my blessing, my blessing."

Almost

The couple standing next to baked beans are arguing. Rachel could tell, even though it was in a 'gritted teeth' sort of way. His back is ramrod-straight, neck muscles twitching, controlling, dominant, while she stands with shoulders hunched, submissive. Because of them she thinks of Neil – for the first time in a long while.

It was a hot pleasant afternoon; they had been sifting through the papers for her college notes for next day in class, sitting lazily at the kitchen table over endless cups of tea, and a few ice-cold glasses of wine. The window was flung open, life was very peaceful between them.

The look on his face made Rachel truly believe the words from his mouth. He had suddenly taken up both her hands in his and told her that, yes, she was quite right, and that they really should be living together now. It was because he never said things lightly that she held his eyes with her own and listened intently as he promised her that her would leave his wife and come to live with her.

Neil – all Greenpeace and conservation, geology and life forces, though Rachel. You said you needed me because I got you, I listened to you, met you halfway. You said I was your equal on so many levels, that we were on a par and that you had now found the courage, through me, to change your life. That you were prepared, suddenly to let go of the reigns that had always formed our relationship.

The couple shopping have moved along a bit to kitchen rolls. He's actually clutching her elbow now as if trying to steer her along the isles, perhaps to a place where he could really let rip at her. She thinks it's mean, pinching hold of her elbow like that.

Neil had held her hands and expressed his fears of getting old before her – that he might become vulnerable to her, that might not be able to come to her without his old familiarities. On reflection, it was a repeated dance, two steps forwards, and three steps back. But he said it was 'now or never' and so they agreed that he would leave his wife and his old life, on the following Saturday.

They sat together then for a long time with arms around each other and wept. Wept for joy, wept for fear, wept for the changes to come. Looking back, maybe for the changes that were never to come.

On Saturday Rachel woke early, alerted to the new life just ahead of her. She cleaned and tidied the flat, put things away, changed the bed, and became more and more gloriously self-absorbed in Neil's certain arrival into her life.

She felt so proud of him because he had finally understood that boring familiarity was incomparable to the adventures of the spirit and body. All they really needed was each other and a sprinkling of luck. Her heart began to sing as she mentally embraced giving up her space for him, opening up the secret chambers of her heart and banishing the loneliness previously felt every time he left.

Restless and with the time still far too early, she went for a walk into the village despite the rain. One of the many things they had in common, walking. She walked remembering a rainy afternoon in a disused tin mine, of all places – geologists! Just the two of them, noses dripping from the rainwater as they kissed passionately in the semi-darkness.

Rachel went into the supermarket for fresh milk for his tea and that's when she saw him and his 'familiarity' wrapped up in a bright blue raincoat, headscarf and sensible shoes. He was picking out tins of soup. High back, ramrod-straight, dominant, she slightly hunched, submissive. She knew then he would not leave his wife… and knew as she watched the submissive yet powerful brand of his wife's 'familiarity' at work that she had lost.

No doubt he would have turned up much later in the day, apologised to Rachel with his eyes full of tears – again – but she wasn't going to wait for that. So she went out on the town, to forget – well, almost.

Mother's Last Christmas

It was on a chilly December afternoon that Harry finally made up his mind – he had to change things.

Collar pulled tight around his thick neck, hair wild and uncombed lashing at his large ruddy face, he had begun the long, familiar walk up the hill from the village, laden with the rucksack and two carrier bags in each hand. She had to go.

Mother was to blame for his utter misery; she had dominated him for over forty years now with her keen eye and sharp tongue. What chance had he of ever living his own life as long as she was around?

His darkening face set in grim determination, Harry battled his way up the hill, knuckles white from the whipping wind and from the fierce rage growing stronger from within. He opened the creaking old gate that led to the cottage just as a car went speeding past him, making him jump.

Turning momentarily towards the sound he glimpsed the fair hair and smiling face, half hidden behind the misty windscreen, of Janet Macey, the doctor's receptionist. She hadn't seen him, just whizzed past, but he still felt his heart leap with joy. She was so lovely and the only time he got to see her was once in a blue moon when he went to the surgery for some minor ailment. But on these rare occasions Janet always asked him how he was, as if she actually meant it! It was the kindness in her, that's all.

He had never even entertained the idea of inviting her home – how could he with *her* there? If he were a free man though, then perhaps, just perhaps. Hurrying up the small, wet flagstones and quickly into the cottage, Janet Macey invading his thoughts had slowly but surely become the powder keg that fuelled his determination to free himself.

The fire had burned steadily down to just a few glowing embers by the time he entered the living room. Two chairs sat in front of the open fireplace, shabby and threadbare – part of Harry's life for as long as he could remember. He sat down heavily in his and turned to glance at his mother sitting in hers.

How old and white she looked, wrapped in that threadbare blanket of hers, her thin cruel mouth in a permanent sneer. Long bony face so pinched, so without love. She began to moan, about the time he had taken to go to the village – as she always did – and she told him to rake the fire up again because she was freezing; her voice rattling on and on in his head – how he hated her in that moment.

Years before, when he was only a few years old, he could recall standing behind her skirts in the hallway as she stood facing the Coalman, raging at him about his prices, shaking her fist at him, telling him to get lost and never come back. No wonder no one in the village had liked them.

They never had callers to the cottage unless it was debt collectors, and the most painful memory of all were the other children calling him names and that his mother was a witch, 'skin-flint'. They would jeer at him until the very tips of his ears turned red with shame and embarrassment. He had felt the hot salty tears run down his face on many occasions on the walk back up the hill to the cottage.

That was before she had decided to keep him out of school altogether; in those days people got away with it. In time no one called at their house. She had managed to scare away most of his friends from school with lies about him being ill and anyone that knocked on the front door became the enemy, someone to be feared as they were usually demanding money. She drummed it into him that it was her and him against the world, that the world was a truly evil place, but that his place was with her and that she would keep him safe, at home.

Then began the teenage years. Instead of having fun and being free like his friends were, he spent every waking hour fetching and carrying for his demanding mother. She used a nasty mix of blackmail and threats, telling him he was delinquent, that no one would ever love him the way she did and she was never satisfied. Why did he take so long? Where had he been? Why did he buy the most expensive butter? If he had ever dared answer back he paid for it with slaps and even a black eye. And later she would throw tantrums if she found out he had been walking a girl home, telling him he was a wilful sinful boy, just like his father had been.

He had grown so used to living with her temper and her demands that he now felt like a crippled man. The lines between reality and fantasy often blurred his view of the world, the more isolated they had become. What was a normal life? Harry had often wondered. She had disempowered him, leaving him nothing more than a puppet whose strings she could constantly pull.

Later that evening as the dark descended, the little kitchen windows threw huge jumping shadows from his movements into the frosty brambled patch of garden outside. Harry looked at the grey shabby work surfaces, peeling paint and swollen Formica coverings in utter despair. He just couldn't live like this anymore. He reached under a table and pulled a half full bottle of cheap brandy on top of it, lifting it to his lips he drank viciously and deeply, his mind focused on nothing but his freedom. He drank several more times from the bottle before flicking off the light in the kitchen and entering the front room, the long handled axe firmly in his hand.

Janet Macey had in fact seen Harry but had pretended not too – she didn't feel comfortable with the man. There was something not quite right with him and the last thing she needed was to have him gazing at her in the way he did, when she was already late home from work. However, her better, professional side had later decided she would in fact turn the car around and go back just to check up on him, see if he was all right. He had looked quite startled as she had driven past, frightened almost and it lay nagging at her slightly. She had often wondered how he got on living in such a remote spot, almost in the side of a hill with no neighbours for miles and nothing but the sharp sweep of the valley to the back of the cottage. Perhaps he was neglecting himself – she would call in on him on her way back to the village, once she had seen to her husband's evening meal.

Janet promised her husband she would only pay a quick call, just to check up on the poor man and that she would be home in time for the news. She then started her cold engine up again and slowly backed the car out of the driveway.

The sharp winter air caught her breath after the heat of the house as she drove back towards the steep hill where Harry lived, thoughts of what the inside of the house must be like playing on her mind. She had the lights on full beam as she swung around the last curve of the lane and the powerful lights fell squarely on the big dark figure of a man on the other side of a small wired fence, carrying something across his shoulders, something draped in what looked like an old blanket. It was Harry, she could see that much. There was no mistaking the size of the man but what was he doing in the semi darkness? She slowed the car right down and leaned over the steering wheel in order to get a better view and that's when she saw the strands of cotton wool white hair hanging out of the blanket that lay awkwardly draped over one huge shoulder.

It took quite a few months for Harry to get things clear in his head. At first he had completely broken down when the policemen came with Janet and he admitted to what he had done straight away, going quietly with them in their car. The confusion came later when they kept telling him he hadn't murdered his mother, when he knew only too well that he had – he even gave them his axe to prove it!

It was when they told him that he couldn't have murdered her, because she had in fact already been dead for several years that it all slowly began to make sense to him.

With carefully chosen words, the psychiatrist explained that she was only really still alive inside his head, not in the 'real world'. He had been so damaged by her, they told him gently, that he thought she was still alive; but the voice he kept hearing wasn't hers at all but one that he had adopted as part of his identity.

It was rather too much for him to completely understand, but one thing he could finally grasp was that he was now, for the first time in his life, a free man.

Loss Adjusting

At first there is just numbness. Nothing and nowhere is safe any more. All things once familiar – acquaintances, friends, even family members – somehow have altered, are no longer to be entirely trusted. The love seen in a smile now has an alter ego; the love felt in the heart has been mortally wounded, invaded and rendered utterly vulnerable. The pain has become a reality, once thought to be understood, but not really, not until now. There is no medicine to stop it from hurting. It will just take its course and that could mean years, or even the rest of your life.

You wake up and it's like a sudden jerk from a car that has had to slam on the brakes. You are jolted into the pain, as if the pain is a person standing right in front of you, two arms held wide open to ensure you enter that kingdom fully.

You wake up and the sun is shining through your bedroom window, but it's a different colour now. 'Food?' – no thanks. 'Wine?' – yes please, but it doesn't numb the pain. Just takes the edge off slightly, then begins to terrify you as it makes you even more vulnerable to the thoughts in your head. Somehow setting adrift an already loose heart.

The night Ruth passed away, her daughter Jayne sat with her for several hours and they 'talked'. Later when she was no longer there, Jayne put on her mother's nightgown and eased her feet into those oh-so-familiar slippers. She lay down on her mum's sofa and tried to close her mind to the reality that had been so suddenly forced upon her.

Letters expressing sorrow she often read, staring at them through blurry eyes, but their content did not help her at first. In fact, at first they only served to annoy and anger her. It was as if someone else, outsiders, were announcing information most personal to her, factual, but denied as if this information were somehow wrong. They were just telling her the truth – but she didn't want to hear it.

Jayne was now in Ruth's bedroom. Going through the wardrobe her smell fills the air in powerful waves as she takes out the dresses and scarves, shoes and swimsuits, to distribute them or pack them away in boxes. The final journey to the charity shop. Ruth could surely, even at this stage, burst through the door and tell her off for touching her lovely clothes. So the knife that is the pain stabs her heart at every possible opportunity, a shared memory with her sister, a brightly coloured scarf, a forgotten photograph? Slash, slash, slash.

The constant phone calls for Ruth from those who didn't yet know and the endless search for numbers and information about those unknown, yet to tell. Jayne came across a handwritten entry in a private diary – about her. Should she weep or laugh at the comment? She began, in fact, a whole new relationship – one that simply could not have come about during the living years. Entries in diaries for future dates and events sent her down a tunnel of impossibility. She would try and imagine her mother at these events, picture the dress Ruth would choose, the chatter and the excitement she would have felt. This was like embarking on a journey of discovery, discovering what she had now lost and discovering all the things she didn't even know about the one who has gone elsewhere.

"This circle of life that we travel on has a beginning and an end; it's the bit in the middle that's the hardest part," Jayne shouted to the bedroom in the empty house that had been their sanctuary for so long.

Twelve years have slipped by and Jayne refuses to wash that slender nightgown and still has those familiar slippers. Occasionally, at special times, she puts on her mum's green Biba eye shadow, wears her rings and sprays what's left of her perfume around the room. She even saw her go past the window once.

These have not been easy years, Jayne reflects, as gently she sips her glass of Sauvignon Blanc, a nice one from New Zealand where she had been living since the devastation of her loss. Now she'd gone back to the village in Gloucestershire, where she had spent the happiest years of her life with her best friend, her mum, dear Ruth.

The years drift across her mind and she ponders on this one and that one: *I have no regrets, no guilt, we enjoyed so much together, I did everything I could for her*, and yet…

I wish I had held her eyes more with mine – more fully, for longer. I wish I had fully appreciated her concerns about having no money and no security as she got older. These little things aside we were okay. Very close, very loving, truly. I was lucky – some people never get that close. Some people sit in their doctor's surgery weeping for their lost relationships with parents and their parents aren't even dead. You do develop a new relationship with the one you have 'lost', that's definitely true.

I walk through the park each morning on my way to work and there is a rose garden planted there. She is in each rose, each gently swaying branch of the trees, in the birdsong. I have seen her walk past my window, I catch the side of her face in a crowd, seen her step, her hands, her arms, her smile, her hair, in a hundred strangers. I feel her inside my heart, my eyes are now her eyes, to look out from me and back into the world again whenever she chooses. She is in the shape of my hands and fingers, but she is also in my memories and awareness, my tone of voice, the expression in my eyes. I mould and meld myself into her until we almost become like one. I absolutely refuse to lose her, why should I?

I walk into the heart of the little village she lived in and as I turn and peer down the narrow road I can see her still, hand in the air gently waving to me as she makes her way up the pavement to meet me. I wave to her as she stands behind the glass doors of the art gallery I walk past each morning. When I close my eyes at night, if I want to see her, I simply ask her if I can 'see her'. I have dreams in which I am totally lucid and she comes to me. I tell her that I know it's just a dream, but would she mind staying for a while with me?

She never minds.